DOCTOR GRUNDY'S UNDIES

DAWN McMILLAN
ILLUSTRATED BY ROSS KINNAIRD

DOVER PUBLICATIONS, INC.
MINEOLA, NEW YORK

Doctor Grundy lost his undies.
His new ones, a larger size,
with tiger stripes and tiger eyes.

He hung them on the line to dry.

The wind blew,

the wind blew ...

and they flew into the sky.

Twirling, whirling, feeling free,
colors bright for all to see.
In the breeze, over the trees,
past the hedge, over the edge,

along the beach, out of reach,
over the quay and out to sea!

They rode the waves, the crest, the dip.

A pirate ship!

"Lower the boats! Row them fast.

We have treasure! Yes! At last!"

"I do declare, new underwear!"
said Pirate Captain Hook.
"Yo ho ho! Way to go!
I love this boxer look!"

The captain washed the undies
and hung them out to dry.
The wind blew,

the wind blew ...

and the undies fluttered high.

The quartermaster wanted them.
The bosun wanted them.
The navigator wanted them.
The cook wanted them.
The cabin boy wanted them.

But the first mate got 'em!

"Give 'em back or you'll walk the plank!"
was the captain's cry.

But the wind blew,

the wind blew ...

and ... blimey ...

did those undies fly!

They knew where they were going ...

to find someone good at sewing.

A lucky flight to land just right,

where tailors stitch so fine.

A seam or two to look brand new ...
then someone said, "They're mine!"

"I'll add a ribbon ... stitch a bow ...
... perhaps a tiny silver heart ..."

The undies knew they had to go!

LUCKILY ...

The wind blew,

the wind blew ...

and out the window the undies flew.

Twirling, whirling, free once more,
they headed toward a distant shore.

A land of highland, lake and glen
where pleated skirts are worn by men.

I'll wear them under m' kilt tonight.
See ... these ol' undies are getting tight."

The bagpipes hummed.

The drummers drummed.

The wind blew,

the wind blew ...

Then ...
Donald's new undies fell down!

They tripped him up, they tore asunder.
The crowd cheered. What a blunder!

"Donal',
Donal'
Where's ya trousers?"

The wind blew,
the wind blew ...
and the undies flew at top speed,
OUT OF THERE!

Twirling, whirling, feeling free,

heading home across the sea.

Danger over, adventure done,

the underpants had had their fun!

Doctor Grundy found his undies
tangled on the line.

"My underwear! My favorite pair!
A little fade, a little wear,
a line of stitching to repair ...
but otherwise they're fine."

Doctor Grundy washed his undies.
He hung them on the line.

The wind blew,

the wind blew ...

ABOUT THE AUTHOR

Ahoy there me hearties! I'm Dawn McMillan from down by the sea on the Coromandel Peninsula in New Zealand. Unfortunately I don't have a pet parrot as most pirates do, but I do have a pet husband and a pet cat living with me. I write lots of different things: fiction and nonfiction, poetry, stories for school readers and stories for picture books. Sometimes my work is serious, sometimes it's just for fun. This one is just for fun. Enjoy!

ABOUT THE ILLUSTRATOR

Gidday, I'm Ross Kinnaird. I'm an illustrator and a graphic designer and I live in Auckland. When I'm not illustrating a book, or being cross with my computer, I enjoy most activities to do with the sea. I love visiting schools to talk about books and drawing. (I've been known to draw some really funny cartoons of the teachers!)

Bibliographical Note

This Dover edition, first published in 2019, is an unabridged republication of the work originally published by Oratia Media Ltd., Auckland, New Zealand, in 2014. This book is copyright. Except for the purposes of fair reviewing, no part of this publication may be reproduced or transmitted in any form or by any means, whether electronic, digital, or mechanical, including photocopying, recording, any digital or computerized format, or any information storage and retrieval system, including by any means via the Internet, without permission in writing from the publisher. Infringers of copyright render themselves liable to prosecution.

International Standard Book Number

ISBN-13: 978-0-486-83248-7
ISBN-10: 0-486-83248-1

Manufactured in the United States by LSC Communications
83248102 2020
www.doverpublications.com